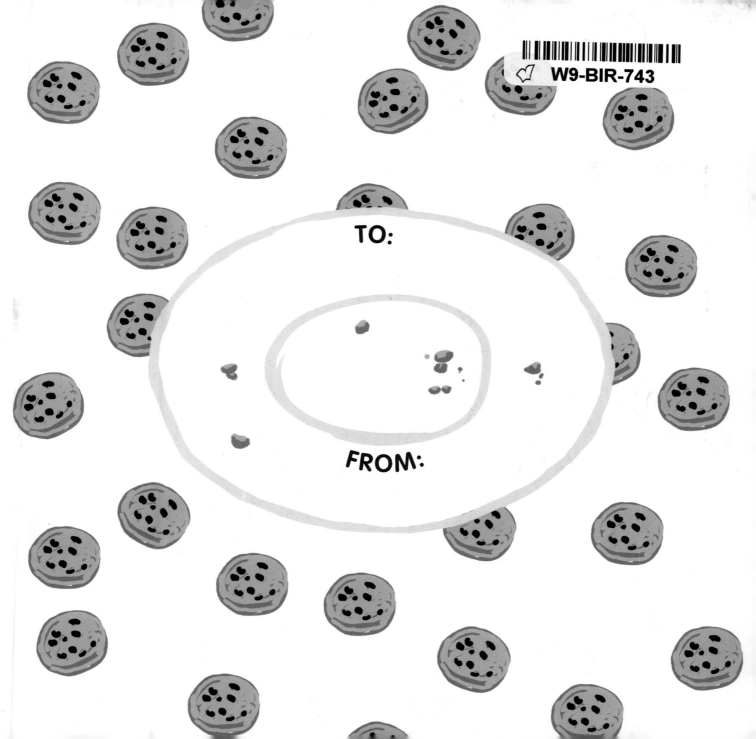

TO:

FROM:

Cookies for Elmo

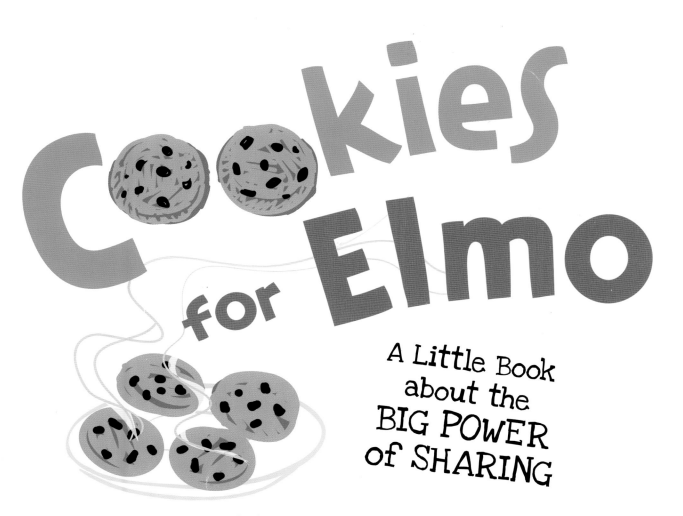

A Little Book about the BIG POWER of SHARING

words by Erin Guendelsberger

pictures by Ernie Kwiat

sourcebooks
wonderland

Two good friends are having fun one bright and happy day.

Elmo shares with Cookie Monster and they play, play, play!

Elmo's favorite rubber ball is HUGE and RED and ROUND!

He tosses it to Cookie, saying, "Keep it off the ground!"

Cookie Monster grabs the ball and bops it up and down.

He uses hands and feet and head to bounce it all around.

He throws the big ball up, up, UP—so high into the air.

He's having such an awesome time! He's glad that Elmo shared.

The two friends played with Elmo's toys till Cookie had to go.

Elmo shared his favorite things and helped their friendship grow.

Cookie thinks about the things that *he* could maybe share.

So how can he show Elmo that he also really cares?

COOKIES! Yes! His favorite thing will make the perfect gift.
Cookie will rush home to make TWO batches, extra swift.

Mix, mix, mix. Then *bake, bake, bake.* And next the cooling rack.

The cookies are so plump and round…the perfect monster snack.

Oh no! He ate the cookies. Every morsel. Every crumb.

Those were Elmo's cookies! What has Cookie Monster done?

He meant to share the cookies, but they looked so good and sweet.

Cookie couldn't help it! He just had to *eat, eat, eat*.

Cookie makes another batch and then he steps away.

This time around, he tells himself, "No more for me today."

Once they're ready, Cookie stacks the goodies on a plate.

He leaves for Elmo's right away—no time to hesitate!

On the way to Elmo's house, there's Bert, and Ernie too!

Cookie says hello and tells them what he's off to do.

They both agree that Elmo's going to love the tasty treat.

Sharing something special with a friend just can't be beat.

Left foot. Right foot. Left foot. Right foot. On and on he walks. Soon he's close to Elmo's house—it's just a few more blocks! The cookies look so yummy, but he knows they're not for him. "Me want cookies!" Cookie says, "but me must not give in."

Cookie takes a breath and tries to think of something new.

Like math! He knows that you get four if you add two and two.

So if he shares four cookies, will he still get two to eat?

Or, once he shares the cookies, will they *all* be Elmo's treat?

Maybe he should eat one now and give away just three.
Elmo won't miss one small cookie. Wouldn't you agree?

Or maybe he should eat two cookies, saving two to share.

Half and half, straight down the middle. Doesn't that seem fair?

Oh no! He ate them all—again!—before he reached the house.
All that's left are cookie crumbs too small to feed a mouse.
There's nothing now that he can share. He's eaten all he had.
Cookie starts to walk back home, alone and feeling sad.

Bert and Ernie, at the park, are reading in the shade.

They stop to ask if Elmo liked the goodies Cookie made.

He has to tell them that *he* ate the sweets himself instead.

"Me no can control me-self!" he says and hangs his head.

Bert and Ernie understand how tough it is to share,
even if you're trying hard to show someone you care.
When it's a thing you *really* love, you want it just for you,
but when you share with someone else, you're sharing friendship too.

Perhaps instead of baking first and sharing when he's done, he could bake *with* Elmo. That would make the sharing fun! "A great idea!" Cookie Monster says and claps his hands. He runs home to call Elmo—SO excited for their plans!

Elmo's fun to work with—he and Cookie have a blast!

They mix and bake together and then share the treats at last.

Seeing Elmo smile and laugh makes Cookie happy too.

Even if it's hard sometimes, it's fun to share with you!

Monster Chocolate Chip Cookies

Makes 4 to 6 Monster Cookies (about 30 small cookies)

Ingredients

I cup plus 2 tablespoons all-purpose flour

½ teaspoon baking soda

½ teaspoon salt

½ cup (I stick) butter, softened

¼ cup granulated sugar

½ cup packed brown sugar

½ teaspoon vanilla extract

I large egg

I cup semi-sweet chocolate chips

I cup chopped walnuts or pecans (optional)

Step 1. Ask a grown-up to preheat the oven to 375°F.

Step 2. Combine flour, baking soda, and salt in a small bowl and set it aside.

Step 3. Beat butter, granulated sugar, brown sugar, and vanilla extract in a large mixing bowl, until creamy.

Step 4. Add the egg and beat well.

Step 5. Gradually beat in flour mixture.

Step 6. Stir in chocolate chips (and chopped nuts, if desired).

Step 7. For MONSTER cookies, form dough balls about 3 inches in diameter (about ¼ cup), arrange on an ungreased baking sheet, and flatten slightly. For small cookies, drop teaspoonfuls of dough on an ungreased baking sheet.

Step 8. Ask a grown-up to put the baking sheet in the oven and bake for 9 to 11 minutes or until golden brown.

Step 9. Cool on baking sheets for 5 minutes and then gently move the cookies to a wire rack to cool completely (Monster Cookies can be fragile).

Step 10. Enjoy! **OM-NOM-NOM-NOM-NOM!**

Cover and internal design © 2020 by Sourcebooks

Cover illustrations © Sesame Workshop

Text by Erin Guendelsberger

Illustrations by Ernie Kwiat

Sourcebooks and the colophon are registered trademarks of Sourcebooks.

Published by Sourcebooks Wonderland, an imprint of Sourcebooks Kids

P.O. Box 4410, Naperville, Illinois 60567–4410

(630) 961-3900

sourcebookskids.com

Source of Production: 1010 Printing Asia Limited, North Point, Hong Kong, China

Date of Production: June 2020

Run Number: 5018858

Printed and bound in China.

OGP 10 9 8 7 6 5 4 3 2 1

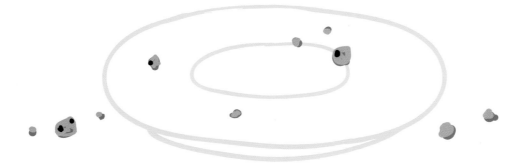

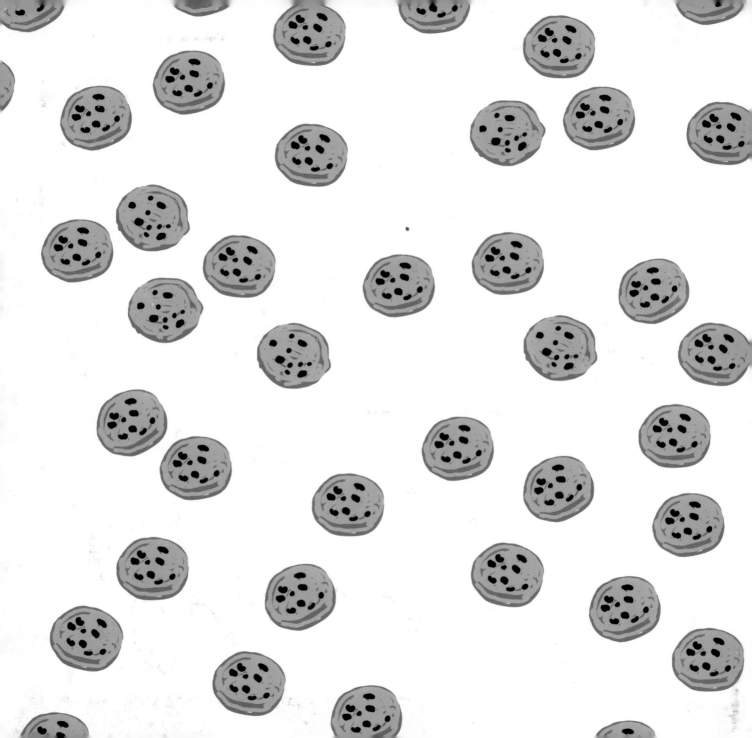